Curious George® DiSCOVERS the Ocean

Adaptation by Bethany V. Freitas

Based on the TV series teleplay
written by Bruce Akiyama

Houghton Mifflin Harcourt

Boston New York

Photographs on front cover and pages 3, 7, 13, 15, 16 (bottom), 19, 23, and 24
courtesy of HMH/Alex Mustard.
Photographs on page 11 courtesy of HMH/Lazaro Ruda.
Top photograph on page 16 courtesy of HMH/Carrie Garcia.
Other images courtesy of HMH.
With special thanks to Carrie Garcia and René Preston.

For information about permission to reproduce selections from this book, write to
Permissions, Houghton Mifflin Harcourt Publishing Company, 215 Park Avenue South,
New York, New York 10003.
ISBN: 978-0-544-45424-8 paper-over-board
ISBN: 978-0-544-43065-5 paperback
Design by Susanna Vagt
www.hmhco.com
Printed in China
SCP 10 9 8 7 6 5 4 3 2 1
4500515620

George was a good little monkey and always very curious. Do you want to hear about the time George discovered the ocean? It's hard to believe, but the story starts in the sky.

George had always dreamed of flying, so this was his lucky night.

"Sorry to pick you up so late," Professor Wiseman said. "But a miniature weather satellite just crashed from space. It needs to be found right away, and I think you can help."

Did you know . . .

there are satellites above earth? They take pictures of how the clouds move. Weather scientists, called meteorologists, use this information to guess when storms will come. You've probably seen satellite photos on weather reports on TV or online.

George and the man with the yellow hat watched from the helicopter as their house got smaller and smaller below. They passed the city, the country, and the beach. Soon they were flying over the ocean. Guess who spotted the ship first?

"Yes, George. There's the Einstein-Pizza research ship just ahead!" the man said.

Professor Einstein and Professor Pizza looked worried. They explained the situation to George.

"The satellite splashed down close by, but no one is sure exactly where. It might have broken in the crash!"

That doesn't sound good, does it? What if the information and photographs the satellite had gathered were lost?

"Should we help them look for it?" the man asked.

George couldn't wait to begin.

Did you know . . .

a research ship is a floating laboratory? Some are designed for day trips, but others are home to researchers for weeks or months. Polar research ships can even sail through frozen seas. Can you imagine being captain of a ship that can move through ice? Where would you go if you were?

If they were going to search the ocean floor for the satellite, they would need to take Pizza and Einstein's submarine. First a helicopter and now a sub! Today was turning into a big adventure.

Did you know . . .

sub is short for *submarine*? Subs can travel underwater. Most subs are long and rounded on both ends, which helps them to move easily through the water. Subs can be even smaller than the one George rode in, with room for only one person to travel for a few hours. Some subs are longer than 500 feet and can stay underwater for up to six months. How would you pass the time on a submarine ride that lasted half a year?

Explore further:

Sonar uses sound waves to "see" objects underwater. The sonar in George's sub sends out sound waves. It can find the satellite underwater by reading the way the sound waves bounce off objects nearby and return to the ship.

Reflected sound waves

Sound waves from ship

Test it out!

Sonar is invisible, but here's how you can see waves: Fill a large bowl with a few inches of water. Use an eyedropper or a bottle with a spout to pour a single drop of water from six inches above the bowl. Do you see the way the water ripples away from the drop in all directions? That's how sonar moves too!

What do you think George saw through the sub's windows? There were so many things to look at! Fish, plants . . .

"Okay, George," the man said. "Keep your eyes peeled for that satellite."

George tried to pay attention. Soon the submarine's sonar began to beep. Had they found the satellite already?

"That's not the satellite, George," Professor Wiseman said. "Look!"
The sonar had found a giant sea turtle!

Did you know . . .

giant sea turtles, or leather-back turtles, are the largest of all turtles? They can live for more than fifty years. Leatherbacks are found all over the world. Males never leave the ocean, but a female swims up onto a beach every two to three years to lay eggs in the sand. She'll be gone by the time the baby sea turtles hatch, but they know to head for the water as soon as they climb out of their shells.

It wasn't long before the sonar found the real satellite.

"We're getting close," Professor Wiseman said. "But hold on.
We have a problem. The satellite is inside that coral reef!"

Oh, no! There was only one way into the reef—through a tiny passage. The sub was much too big to fit. George was so disappointed.

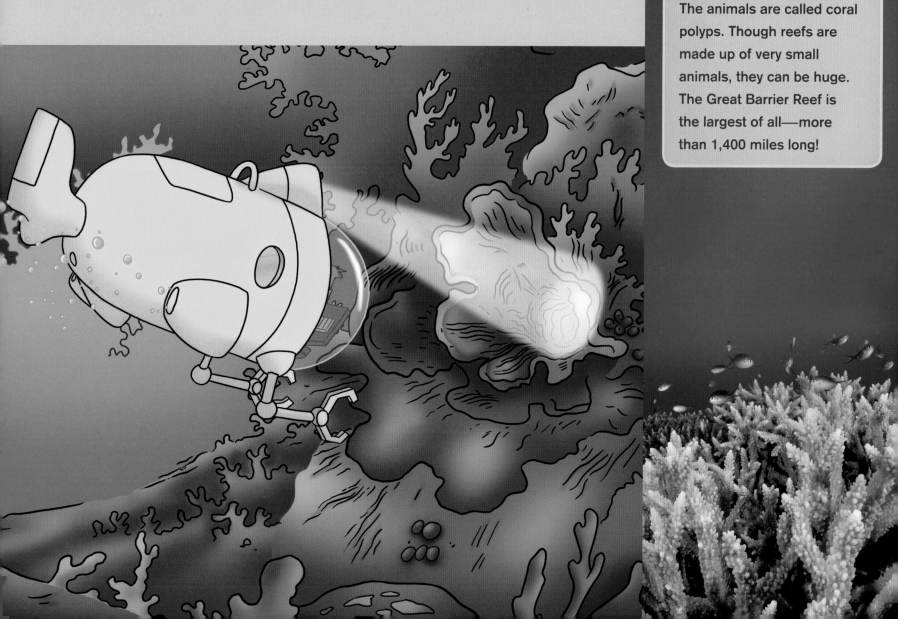

Did you know . . .

coral may look like plants and rocks, but it's actually made up of tiny animals? The animals are called coral polyps. Though reefs are made up of very small animals, they can be huge. The Great Barrier Reef is the largest of all—more than 1,400 miles long!

The team returned to the research ship to make a new plan. If the sub was too big to get into the reef, they'd need something smaller. Do you have any ideas?

George had one. *He* was small enough to fit through the opening! With a scuba suit, George could swim in, explore the coral reef, and get the satellite!

George's scuba suit fit just right.

"Your helmet contains a camera, microphone, and headphones. This locator will flash when you're close to the satellite," Professor Wiseman explained. "We'll be able to see you on our monitor and speak to you the whole time. Are you ready?"

George was ready—and excited!

The swim fins helped George swim fast! He swam over and around the coral reef until he spotted the opening.

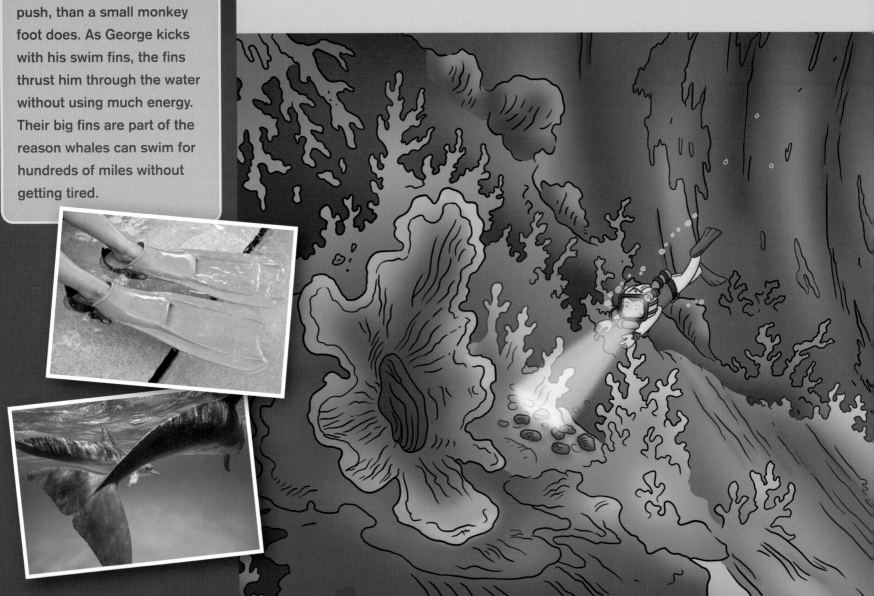

"YOU FOUND THE OPENING, GEORGE!" He could hear Professor Wiseman's voice loud and clear through the speakers in his helmet. *"YOU SHOULD BE ABLE TO SWIM RIGHT THROUGH."*

Once he was inside, George couldn't believe his eyes! Can you believe how many animals live inside the coral reef?

With so many new creatures swimming around him, George never expected to run into someone he recognized! Exploring the coral reef was so much fun that George almost forgot why he was there . . . until he was distracted by a beeping sound. What could it be?

His locator! It was flashing. *"YOU'RE GETTING CLOSE TO THE SATELLITE, GEORGE!"* Professor Wiseman said. George and his new friend swam deeper.

George looked. And looked. The satellite must be here somewhere.

Suddenly, George noticed something strange: Shadows swirled around him on the ocean floor. Shark-shaped shadows. George was frightened. He wasn't sure if sharks and monkeys were friends.

Explore further . . .

Like many ecosystems, the coral reef has a food chain made up of plants, herbivores, and carnivores. Here's how it works:

Reef sharks = carnivores. *They eat other animals, such as parrotfish.*

Parrotfish = herbivores. *They eat plants such as algae.*

Algae = plants. *They get their energy from sunlight.*

As you may have guessed, monkeys are not part of the coral reef food chain.

"DON'T WORRY, GEORGE. THOSE SMALL REEF SHARKS AREN'T HUNGRY. THE CORAL REEF SUPPLIES THEM WITH ALL THE FOOD THEY NEED," Professor Wiseman explained.

What a relief! George was so distracted by the sharks that
it took him a moment to notice what was behind him. It was
right there! He had finally found the satellite!

Professor Wiseman flew her helicopter over the reef and lowered a rope down to the sea floor. George grabbed on, and he and the satellite rode out of the water, up to the helicopter, and back to the research ship.

George was happy that he found the satellite. But still, if it was broken, all that work and searching would be for nothing.

When they got back to the ship, Einstein and Pizza checked the satellite.

"It's in great shape!" Professor Pizza said.

"Not a scratch on it!" shouted Professor Einstein.

The research was saved! All thanks to George.

"Ahoy, George!" they called to him from the ship. They wanted to celebrate! But what do you think George was doing?

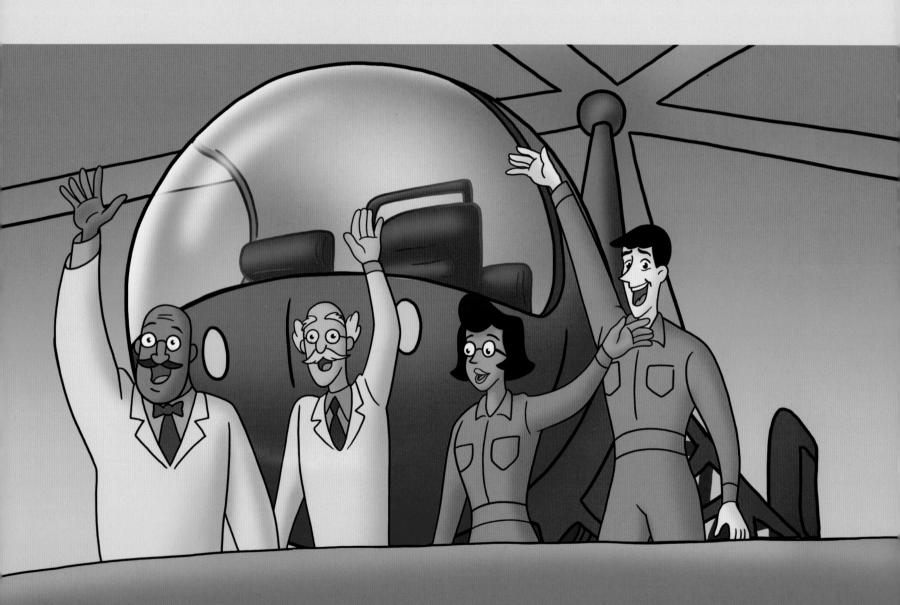

It had been quite a day. George got to fly in a helicopter, and that was fun. But he decided swimming in the ocean was even better . . . because in the sky there are no sea turtles.

Reflected sound waves

Sound waves from ship

Exploring Sonar

George and his friends used sonar to find the satellite on the ocean floor. Listening to sound waves bouncing off objects underwater helps oceanographers figure out how far they are from what they're looking for—coral reefs, trenches, or lost satellites! You can guess where you are in a room with your eyes closed the same way.

Test it out!

You'll need . . .

- **an empty room, like your garage or the school gym**

- **your ears**

- **your loudest voice**

Stand in the empty room, close your eyes, tune up your ears, and make some noise! How does the echo sound when you stand in the middle of the room? How about when you stand in the corner or close to a wall? How does the echo change based on your position?

Echoes sound longer when you are farther away from a wall because it takes longer for the sound waves to reach the wall and bounce back to your ears. Sonar works the same way. Oceanographers use it to map the ocean floor. If the sound waves bounce back quickly, the floor is close. If they take longer, the floor is farther away and the water is deeper.

Who's Hungry?

Can you sort the organisms into these categories:
carnivores, herbivores, and **plants?**

ALGAE	GRAIN	MOUSE
CLOVER	GRASS	RABBIT
PARROTFISH	HOUSECAT	SHARK
ZEBRA	LION	WOLF

Now can you use the animals to make a food chain for each of these ecosystems?

CORAL REEF

SAVANNAH

FOREST

BACKYARD

Here's an example:

shark < parrotfish < algae = coral reef.

In the corral reef, sharks hunt parrotfish and parrotfish eat algae.

Testing Thrust

Don't believe swim fins helped George swim faster than he could have without them? Test it out for yourself! Fill a bucket, sink, or bathtub with a few inches of water. Gather some flat-ish items of various sizes: a soup spoon, a spatula, a shovel, even your hand. Using a stirring motion, test the resistance of each of the items. Do you notice a difference in resistance, or "drag"? Which items feel like they're giving you the most thrust? Is there a link between an object's shape and the amount of drag you notice?